WHICH Witch's Wand Works?

First published in 2004
by Meadowside Children's Books
This edition published 2010 by Little Bee,
an imprint of Meadowside Children's Books
185 Fleet Street, London EC4A 2HS

A CIP catalogue record for this book is available from the British Library
Printed in Thailand
10 9 8 7 6 5 4 3 2 1

little bee

This is a story about
a witch called Rattle,
a witch called Ricket
and their cat (called Rum)

This is Rattle.
(She has trouble flying
in very strong winds)

Every Friday evening Rattle, Ricket and Rum
sit down to watch their favourite
television programme…

"I could do better than that," said Rattle.

"Well, I could do better than you could," said Ricket.

"Then, I could do better than you can do
better than I could!" snorted Rattle.

"Hah! I can do better than you could do better,
doing better than I can do better
than you DO do better than I can!!!" shouted Ricket.

"Alright! A contest," challenged Rattle.

*"Tongue of toad,
drool of dog.
Turn this witch
into a frog!"*

Poof!

(Well, at least
she was green)

*"Eye of bat and black squid's ink,
'Make my sister start to shrink."*

But Ricket began to blow up
like a balloon and then took
off around the room.

Pop!

HissS

ssssssssssSSSSSS

Ricket finally landed in a heap on her chair.

"Claw of crab and weasel's ear,
Make my sister disappear."

Puff!

Moments later Rattle
disappeared and Ricket
gave a triumphant cackle.

(Ricket is good...
...but not that good.
Rattle hadn't disappeared.
She was clinging to the
top of a nearby flagpole)

" Legs of Spiders..."

" ...shells of snails..."

The witches carried on
and the spells flew back
and forth.

…aaaaaaahhhhhhh!!!!!!!!"

"Where's Rum?!"

One spell had gone wrong and
Rum was now disappearing down
the road in the back of a dustcart.
(amongst the snails, bugs and slugs)

Rattle jumped on her
broomstick and flew
out the window in hot
pursuit.

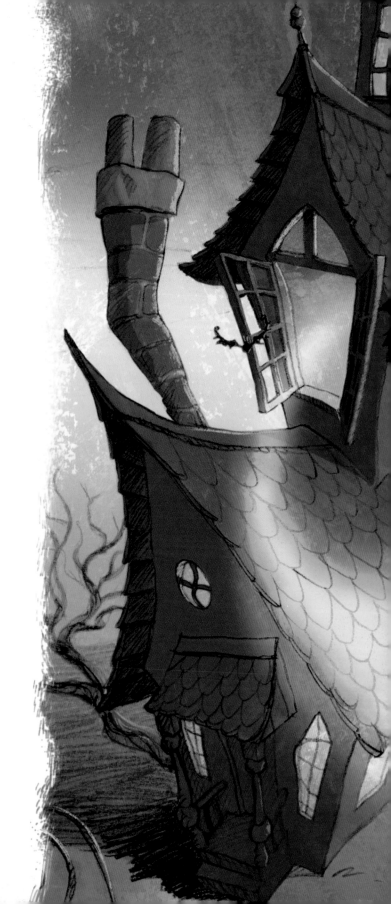

(Ricket? Well she was struggling
to get airborne)

Just as the witches were
catching the
dustcart,
the wind

blew Rattle off
her broomstick.

She tumbled through
the air, landing
with a loud bump
on the windscreen of the dustcart,
which stopped.

Overjoyed they hugged Rum
(but not too close as he smelled of rubbish)

So together they climbed
on to Rattle's broomstick
and flew home.

And to celebrate,
they decided to
have a party…

So now we're back where we started, with Rattle
(Who clears the dancefloor)

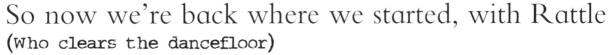

with Ricket
(Who clears the plates)

And Rum…

...(who just clears up)